One Litt

One Little Black Nose

An Adventure

BY

Clare Passingham

Illustrations by Amy Brown

© Clare Passingham, 2015

Published by Upcott Press

All rights reserved. No part of this book may be reproduced, adapted, stored in a retrieval system or transmitted by any means, electronic, mechanical, photocopying, or otherwise without the prior written permission of the author.

The rights of Clare Passingham to be identified as the author of this work have been asserted in accordance with the Copyright, Designs and Patents Act 1988.

A CIP catalogue record for this book is available from the British Library.

ISBN 978-0-9935180-0-3

Book layout and cover design by Clare Brayshaw

Prepared and printed by:

York Publishing Services Ltd
64 Hallfield Road
Layerthorpe
York YO31 7ZQ

Tel: 01904 431213

Website: www.yps-publishing.co.uk

For Arlo and Zachary

Chapter 1

Jack Bennett was finishing his breakfast, in a bit of a daydream as usual. He was slowly licking his porridge spoon of the last traces of sugar. The front door banged as his sister Sally set off for school.

'Jack, do try and hurry for once – Charlie will be waiting!' Jack was always extra slow on a Monday morning.

'Now have you packed up your schoolbag? Homework... dinner-money...your reading book?' His Mum sighed – in another world, his Nan always said.

A few minutes later Jack was at the front door, well wrapped up against the chill winter morning. His Mum kissed him good-bye, and he set off down the road, hurrying a bit now. He was heading for Charlie's house, just round the corner, in Melton Avenue. Charlie was his best friend, and they always walked to school together. He was a chirpy boy, even on those days when he hadn't done his homework. Nothing could dent Charlie's belief that he could get by, whatever turned up. And even the fiercest teacher at school melted a little when faced with his cheeky grin.

Jack swung open the wooden gate and climbed the steps. Charlie lived in a ground floor flat, with a garden shared with an elderly lady in the flat upstairs. Jack pushed hard at the bell. It rang – but no sound came in response. Jack frowned, puzzled. Usually there was the sound of Mrs Munroe's radio, playing cheerful music in the kitchen at breakfast. And Charlie was never one for creeping about quietly: you could hear him a mile off. Jack cautiously lifted the letter-box flap and peered in. No sign of anyone there, and no coats hanging on the peg either. Perhaps Charlie had set off for school early for some reason? Or had to go to see the doctor? Jack shouted through the letter-box as loudly as he could. There was no reply.

Jack dropped his bag: if he stood on tip-toe, he could just see into the front room window. His heart sank when he saw that the room had been cleared of all its usual clutter; even the big rented television that sat in the corner was not there. Jack felt a cold finger of dread running down his back: Charlie and his mother were gone!

Chapter 2

'You're late, Jack Bennett!' Miss Simms said, her pen poised above the register that she had just finished checking.

'I'm sorry, Miss,' Jack replied, in a voice that came out rather choked.

'Why, whatever's the matter, Jack?' Miss Simms turned to look at him with a slight frown on her face. 'Are you all right?'

'It's Charlie, Miss,' Jack replied, 'He wasn't at home when I called there, and I don't know where he's gone.'

'Well, he certainly isn't here,' Miss Simms replied briskly. Jack had seen that already, hopefully scanning the room the moment he opened the class-room door, in case by some miracle, Charlie was sitting in his usual place. She said:

'Well, we'll just have to wait for him to tell us when he's back, won't we? Come and sit down now you're here, Jack.'

So began a very miserable school-day for Jack. Without his friend at the next desk, it seemed to last forever.

At last the end of school arrived, and Jack pulled his coat on and, in a rush, set off for home. The sun was already low in the sky and a mist was settling over the trees. He hurried until he came to the road where Charlie lived. His feet began to feel like lead – a part of him really didn't want to check if Charlie was back, because he felt already that he *knew* he wasn't there. And sure enough, there were no lights on in the flat, and the curtains were still open. So Jack didn't stop to look, but turned towards home.

Jack could hear his mother humming in the kitchen as he pushed at the back door. She turned to greet him.

'How was school today then?' she said.

Jack started to explain about Charlie. But instead of words coming out, he burst into tears. His mother grabbed him in a hug.

'What's happened, Jack?'

Hot tears ran down Jack's face, making a damp patch on his mother's sleeve. He took a deep breath in, and bit his lip – thank goodness Sally wasn't there to see him.

It was some time before he managed to get his story out.

'I'm sure there'll be a simple explanation,' Mrs Bennett said reassuringly, fetching a damp cloth to wipe his face. 'And now,' she said, 'you look like you need a treat.'

She opened the kitchen cupboard and pulled out a box of chocolate biscuits, kept for unexpected visitors. She carefully tipped some onto a plate.

'And when Dad gets back, we'll ask him if he's heard anything – there's not much news he misses in the shop,' she added, helpfully.

Jack managed half a smile, and with a sigh, sat down at the table.

Chapter 3

Jack was upstairs in his bedroom when his dad came home. Mr Bennett worked long hours in the shop, and usually headed straight for his easy chair in the living room to put his feet up with a cup of tea. This time Mrs Bennett gave him her usual peck on the cheek, and then told him about Jack's troubles. They talked for a few moments in low voices, so Jack wouldn't overhear. Mrs Bennett had done the same when Sally had bounced in, straight from her netball practice.

'Try and be sympathetic, Sal,' she had said. 'No teasing, now.' Sally had promised to be helpful, and indeed she was for a day or two.

Mr Bennett went up to Jack's room.

'Mum's told me about Charlie,' he said, poking his head round the door. Jack looked up, but said nothing. 'Do you want me to go over your homework before supper? Give you a hand with those times tables Mum said you had to learn?'

So together they tackled Jack's eight times table before supper. When Mum called them, Dad said:

'Charlie'll be back, don't you worry, Jack. Think – his mum's got a good job at the hospital and Charlie's happy at school here. They won't have left for good, I'm sure of that.'

The next morning, Mrs Bennett had a bit of a struggle to get Jack up. He just slid back down into the bed, and pulled the blankets over his head.

'I don't feel well,' he mumbled from under the bedclothes. Mrs Bennett sat down on the side of the bed.

'Well, what's the matter?' she asked.

'I don't know, I just don't feel well,' he repeated.

'Don't be silly, Jack,' his mum replied, pulling down the sheet so she could get a good look at him. 'You'll feel better after some breakfast. How about it if I make some toast and honey today?'

Jack groaned, but he did sit up, rubbing his head gingerly.

'I wondered,' said Mrs Bennett, thoughtfully, 'if you and I should go down to Charlie's house after school and ask the lady in the flat above if she knows anything about where the Munroes have gone. She might have heard something.'

Jack and Charlie had often seen old Mrs Jones peering out at them from the upstairs window, as they set off for school. To the boys, she seemed very old. She had wispy grey hair and a wrinkled face; they had decided she might be a witch.

'Thanks, Mum,' Jack brightened a little, 'but you'll do the asking?' he added nervously.

So that evening Jack and his mum set off for Charlie's house. Jack had passed it this morning, on his rather reluctant way to school, checking with a hurried glance that there were still no signs of life.

Mrs Bennett stepped onto the lawn for a brief moment to see the empty room for herself, before firmly pressing the bell for the upper flat. There was a long silence before they heard Mrs Jones coming down the stairs, her walking stick rattling on the banisters. Jack stood just behind his mother, as if this might give him some protection, if she really was a witch.

'I'm very sorry to trouble you, Mrs Jones. It's Mrs Bennett – you probably know my husband, from Bennett's Grocery on the main road.'

Mrs Jones nodded and smiled slightly. 'Of course I do, Mrs Bennett, but why the call on such a chilly evening?'

Mrs Bennett explained that they were trying to find out something about the Munroes' sudden disappearance at the weekend.

'Oh, quite a thing, that!' Mrs Jones replied, suddenly animated, 'but we can't just stand here – I'll be catching my death. Come inside, my dears.'

She beckoned them into the hallway, and pulled the front door to.

'I can't tell you why they left, but it was all a bit odd, if you ask me. Perhaps they couldn't pay the rent?' She paused and gave an enquiring look at Mrs Bennett.

'They didn't say a thing beforehand, not to me anyway, but on Sunday, I heard a car pull up in the early morning – must have been about four o'clock – it was still dark as pitch. I heard some voices, so I got out of bed and had a peek from behind the curtains. Well, I thought it might be burglars, Mrs Bennett, you never can be sure, these days!'

Mrs Jones stood there for a moment, shaking her head, her grey hair flying.

'It was a taxi, would you believe! Packed full of stuff – suitcases, big bags, saucepans, even the little 'uns bicycle tied to the back! And then they drove off, and I've heard nothing since. Well, what can you make of it! And Mrs Munroe such a respectable lady – so helpful whenever I needed a hand!'

'Well, it's certainly a mystery, Mrs Jones,' replied Mrs Bennett. 'And I do hope we find out soon. It's very strange! Perhaps they'll write or send a postcard.' she added, turning to Jack, who was still hiding behind her.

Jack's face was a picture of misery. He knew that Charlie had gone for good, if he'd taken his beloved bike with him. He was certain of it now. No more games of football in the park, or having him to stay over when Mrs Munroe was doing a night shift.

Mrs Bennett took one look at Jack and then turned back to the old lady. 'Perhaps you should let the landlord know about this, Mrs Jones. And, you know, Jack is really missing Charlie, so please tell us if you hear anything, won't you?'

'Well, the landlord's certain to be round on Friday, like clockwork, that's for sure!' said Mrs Jones, with a hoarse laugh, 'so I will ask him. And if I hear anything, I'll pass a message onto your husband in the shop, shall I?'

Mrs Jones closed the door behind them after they'd said polite goodbyes. The dusk was deepening and the street lamps were already flickering on. Mrs Bennett took Jack's arm, but neither said a word as they both hurried home.

Chapter 4

Miss Simms was worried about Jack. He was very quiet these days – she had to work hard to get a word out of him. And she was alarmed to see Charlie's place empty every day. Each time she took the register, she said 'Mmm, no Charlie,' and put another cross by his name.

On Friday, she snapped the register shut, and told the class she was going to rearrange their seating. There was a groan from the whole room.

'I'm going to separate you twins, I'm afraid,' she said, looking at Jenny and Beth in the back row.

'Oh, that isn't fair!' they both shouted, jumping up from their seats in indignation. 'We've always been together!'

To tell the truth, Miss Simms had been looking for a while for a chance to move one of them.

Together, they whispered constantly, and she thought there might be more than a bit of cheating going on; they proved the old saying about two heads being better than one.

So Jenny was moved to sit next to Jack, and after a few grumbles, the class had settled. Jack didn't know what to think about the change – it made him feel Charlie was never coming back, and that gave him a sinking feeling in his stomach. But Jenny was friendly, and good at sums, so after a while he began to appreciate someone who could help him, when he was stuck. And perhaps it was better not to have an empty desk beside him.

At the end of the second week, Miss Simms told Jack after the morning break, that the head teacher wanted to see him. Jack's face dropped – it usually meant a telling-off for doing something naughty.

'What for?' he asked in a whisper.

'Don't worry, Jack – she just wants to see you about Charlie, because he's been away for so long,' replied Miss Simms.

So Jack went along the corridor to Mrs Atkins' room and knocked on the door, rather quietly. Mrs Atkins called him in her clear ringing voice – you could always hear her right down the corridor. She was a rather overwhelming person, usually full of enthusiasm, but rather frightening if you had broken school rules. Even though he hadn't, Jack's knees were knocking.

But Mrs Atkins welcomed him in and patted a chair next to her desk, for him to sit down.

'I want to ask about Charlie, Jack,' she said. 'He's missed school for two weeks now. And the school governors, you see, need to know why he's not here. Can you tell me anything you know?'

But Jack couldn't add anything to what he had already told Miss Simms. Except that old Mrs Jones had turned up at his dad's grocery store and said in a loud whisper, that the landlord told her that payment for the rent was left in an envelope in the Munroe's flat. And there had been a note, but only to say sorry for leaving suddenly. So that ruled out problems paying the rent, his dad had said.

Mrs Atkins thanked Jack and added, 'You must be missing Charlie – he was a good friend of yours, wasn't he?' She patted his shoulder and said:

'We're worried too. But he'll turn up, just you wait and see.'

Chapter 5

The following Thursday, Mrs Bennett reminded Jack and Sally they were going to Granddad's house after school. It was her afternoon to help Dad pack up the orders for Friday. Nan and Granddad lived on the other side of town, in Caldecott, in a little redbrick house, where they had retired after running one of the village shops in Drayton.

Mrs Bennett enjoyed her Thursday afternoons. During the week she helped her husband do the accounts, and typed out letters for him, but that didn't get her out of the house: they had the smallest bedroom converted into a kind of office where she worked in free moments. Working in the shop was different. Thursday was early closing day and the time was given over to packing the large boxes with a week's groceries for their customers. First she had to sort out the piles of slips with the orders scribbled on them, and then she and Mr Bennett went through them, with their assistant Nicos running up and down to fetch what was needed from the shelves. Nicos had come to live in Abingdon from Cyprus, a few years' back, and worked part-time in the shop. He was studying at college, to be a doctor, he said.

When they had finished, Mr Bennett and Nicos set to loading the boxes into the van. Mrs Bennett, wrapping a warm scarf round her, set off for home. It was dark already, and there was frost in the air. On the way, she bumped into Marian's mother. Marian was at Jack's school, but two years older. She was a bit of a tom-boy, always out on her bike or climbing trees. Her dad had even built her a tree-house in the big ash tree in their back garden, and she sometimes let Jack and Charlie play there.

So Mrs Bennett wasn't surprised when Marian's mother asked about Charlie. They talked for a while, until Mrs Bennett said:

'Would Marian mind if…' she paused to think of the best way to ask. 'You see, Jack's getting quite difficult to get to school these mornings. He keeps complaining of tummy-ache, you know. I'm sure he's just trying it on, but perhaps if Marian called by on her way to school, he'd snap out of it.'

Marian's mother promised to have a word. So for the next few weeks, Marian called round each morning. Jack sulked at first, but Marian was always ready to chatter, and didn't seem to mind that Jack said nothing much as they walked. It helped a bit that they sometimes talked about Charlie – she missed him too, she said.

Chapter 6

When Jack opened his eyes one morning later that month, he knew at once that something had changed. There was a white glow on the ceiling: he jumped out of bed, and pulled the curtain aside. He couldn't see out at all – the window was quite frosted over, in a delicate icy tracery. Jack Frost's paintings, his Nan called it. Jack rubbed at the window, to clear a tiny hole to see through. Yes! He was right – it had snowed in the night, a heavy fall that transformed the garden. Everything was white and bright, the shrubs bending low with the weight on their branches. Jack didn't wait a moment, and quickly pulled his dressing-gown on and rushed to bang on Sally's door.

'Snow, Sally!' he called and thundered downstairs to find his boots and unlock the back door. His mum came rushing after him before he could get outside.

'Clothes on first!' she cried. She was secretly glad at this show of enthusiasm from Jack – like his old self again.

Jack sighed and climbed back upstairs, and quickly pulled his clothes on – not school uniform of course, not for playing snowballs. Sally and Jack rushed into the untouched snow, Sally shrieking loudly – not at all the grown-up girl she tried to persuade everyone she now was.

After a while, Mrs Bennett called them in to breakfast. She took their sopping gloves, now smelling horribly of wet wool, and hung them above the stove, while dripping wellies were parked on newspaper by the back door.

'You're in luck, Jack,' she said, as she dished out eggs and bacon for them both. 'I've had a phone call from Marian's mum. There's no school for you today – the pipes have burst from the frost last night and there's no heating. And I'm busy today,' she added, 'so you'll have to go over to Nan and Granddad for the day.'

Sally gave her brother an envious look; she would have rather liked to come along too. But of course, she couldn't make a fuss, as she was always telling Jack how much more important her school was than his.

It was quite a long walk to Nan and Granddad's house but Jack knew the way well. The snow crunched and squeaked as he walked along in his boots. For most of the way, the only tracks were from the postman and the milkman. A moment's pang hit him when he saw several snowmen standing in the front gardens as he passed. He and Charlie would have made one together, for the snow was inches thick. Last year they had built one taller than themselves with sticks for arms. It had lasted for more than two weeks before melting away, as there had been a long cold spell that year.

When Jack turned into Caldecott Road his fingers were stiff with cold, and he couldn't feel his toes. So he was glad to reach the little house at the end of the street. There he found Granddad in the front garden with a shovel and a broom, clearing the path of snow.

'It's the best way to keep warm, to my mind!' he laughed, as he stamped his boots and followed Jack into the house.

The two of them were soon unfreezing their hands on Nan's mugs of hot cocoa, with Jack wriggling his feet in front of the kitchen fire.

'He's got something special for you today,' said Nan, nodding in the direction of Granddad. 'You tell him, Joe.'

Granddad said: 'Well, it's a special day, isn't it, you being here all day and with no schoolwork to do.'

'And no Sally to boss you about, either!' Nan added.

'What is it, Granddad?' Jack asked, curious.

'We're going to set up a new section on my train set,' he replied, with a smile.

Granddad's model train set was famous. It was a Hornby one, built in a spare room and it filled the whole space. Granddad was nuts about trains, dragging Nan on holidays for the chance of going on a stretch of steam railway – he'd been on practically every old line in the country: the Settle to Carlisle railway, the Ffestiniog line in Wales, the Bluebell line in Sussex. He had joined a club for steam train enthusiasts. And he tended his own train set as if it were his baby. He had built the sidings, bridges and station buildings himself. He even had a shiny brass engine that rushed round the line, driven by steam heated with a real flame.

So Jack and Granddad spent the day setting up a new section of line, with trees and a level crossing, all carefully painted and set in position. It was messy work, and needed concentration, which helped to take Jack's mind off missing

Charlie. Nan was dragged up from cooking supper to admire it, as the train with its sturdy little engine chuffed around the track.

Granddad and Jack walked home together that afternoon as dusk fell. There were icicles forming over the eaves of many of the houses as the snow-melt froze.

'It'll be cold for a while, I reckon' Granddad had said to Mrs Bennett as he left Jack at home, and set off for the hot supper Nan had waiting for him.

And back at home, after supper when he was enjoying his pipe and cup of tea, he confided in Nan:

'He's missing Charlie badly, that young grandson of ours. It'll take more than my model railway to take his mind off it.'

Chapter 7

The snow had long melted, and crocuses were already showing purple and gold through the damp ground. Mrs Bennett was battling wind and rain, holding her umbrella with two hands as she walked down Ock Street towards a little café. Almost every week, she and her best friend Peggy met for a morning coffee and a chat. She pushed the door open, shaking her wet umbrella as she came in. There was a hum of chatter; the café was popular, famous for its cakes. Peggy was already there, sitting at a table.

'My, what a day!' said Mrs Bennett, as she folded her umbrella and pulled off her raincoat. She sat down with a sigh, as a waitress in a crisp white apron hurried over.

'Is it the usual for you both today?' she asked with a smile. They nodded. 'I won't be a moment then,' she added and hurried off to the kitchen.

Peggy was one of Mrs Bennett's oldest friends. They had known each other since school days. Peggy had lived in London when her children were small, but had moved back to Abingdon recently. So now they met regularly for coffee and a chat.

'How's Jack?' Peggy asked, as soon as the waitress had returned with their pot of coffee and slices of chocolate cake.

'Things are a bit better, I think,' replied Mrs Bennett. 'He's walking to school with Marian Brown now, you know. That means he's easier to get out of the house in the morning. There's not so much complaining of tummy-ache now. But he's still not himself. Miss Simms told me at the last parents' evening that he's not working hard enough – seems to be in a dream all the time.'

She sighed, and Peggy patted her arm.

'I get like that when I'm worrying, so I know how he feels. Perhaps if he had something else to distract him, to take him out of himself.' She thought for a moment, sipping her cup of coffee pensively.

'What about a pet for him?' she said, 'perhaps a rabbit or a guinea pig? My boys had hamsters when we were in our London flat. They were quite sweet and not much trouble, though they do make a racket at night. Jack would have to make a bit of an effort to care for them – you know, cleaning and feeding…. And you can breed them too, but that might be more trouble for you…'

'Well it's certainly an idea,' Mrs Bennett laughed, 'though I'm not keen on the idea of a house full of them! It'll take a bit of thought… but I might look in at the pet shop sometime to see what they have.'

Mrs Bennett had some shopping to do on her way home, and happened to pass the pet shop. She pushed open the door. A pungent smell of mice and damp sawdust filled her nostrils, and a raucous squawk greeted her. It was a Mynah bird, swinging on a little perch suspended from the ceiling. Sorry, no hamsters, the shopkeeper said, but he did have a litter of guinea pigs due in next week. So Mrs Bennett made a mental note to drop by again soon.

She had only just stepped through her front door at home, when the phone rang. It was Nan.

'I've had an idea to cheer Jack up' she said. 'Why don't you ask my sister May if she would have Jack for a few days, in the holidays or next half-term? I'm sure she would enjoy a bit of sightseeing with him. And London would be a bit of a thrill for him, wouldn't it? I mean, there's plenty to see!'

'Mmm,' said Mrs Bennett, 'That's the second good idea I've been given this morning! We'll have to talk it over – I'll let you know.'

There was no more time for pondering – there was shopping to unpack and a pile of ironing to be done before the children came home from school.

That evening, Mr and Mrs Bennett were sitting after supper, cups of hot cocoa on the table beside them.

'Your mum rang today,' Mrs Bennett said.

Mr Bennett looked up – it was unusual for Nan to ring. She was always pretty tongue-tied on the phone.

'What about? No trouble, I hope?' he asked.

'No, not at all,' Mrs Bennett laughed. 'It was about Jack.' She paused to sip her cocoa. 'Well, she suggested we asked Auntie May if Jack could spend time with her in London. Easter holidays would be possible, perhaps. What do you think? It's rather a good idea, I thought.'

'Well...' he paused to look at her across the room, and a smile broke out on his face. ' What a good idea! It'll do Auntie May a power of good too, I'd guess, having a youngster to stay – it'll be a breath of fresh air for her. I'll ring her at the weekend, if I can find a quiet moment. But...' he added, 'perhaps you'd better ask Jack first.'

'Oh yes, I'll do that, of course,' she replied. 'But I heard another good suggestion today – from Peggy. She suggested getting a pet for Jack. A hamster or a guinea pig, she thought. And the man in the pet shop said he was getting some guinea-pigs in soon.'

'Mmm – knowing Jack, he'd lose interest rather quick. Then we'd be left doing the cleaning out – all the work and none of the pleasure! I think it should be something all the family can share, like a cat or a dog, maybe?'

They both agreed to think it over. Cocoa finished, they turned off the lights and headed upstairs for bed.

Chapter 8

It was a rainy evening and almost the end of term. Jack and Sally were both sitting hunched at the dining table, with their homework. Jack was struggling with some hated sums, while Sally was copying a map into her geography notebook, carefully outlining each section of the map with a different colour.

Mrs Bennett had warned them that she would be out for a while. This was unusual for her as she made an effort most days, to be at home when they came in from school. She had left a plate of biscuits and glasses of milk out on the table. These had been scoffed in no time.

Sally was fidgety and kept shooting glances at Jack.

'What's the matter with you?' he asked grumpily.

'Nothing, nothing!' she'd replied hastily. Jack could have sworn she was hiding a grin. Stupid sister, he thought. I wish I had a brother instead, someone like Charlie. Anyone would be better than Sally.

Just then there was a rattle at the back door. It was Mum and Dad together – a surprise, because Mr Bennett was not usually home until much later. The two parents stood in the doorway looking rather sheepish. They were holding a large cardboard box between them; the two children looked on, Jack's mouth falling open at this odd sight.

Then Mrs Bennett coughed slightly and said:

'Jack, we've got something for you – do you want to see?'

Jack looked mystified – was this a trick? He got up slowly and stood staring at each of his parents in turn. Then with a wary expression on his face, he gently lifted the cardboard flap of the box and peered in. There was a moment's silence and then a gasp. Curled up in a rumple of old blankets, there lay a tiny puppy with big brown eyes, his little black nose lifted up, sniffing the air.

'He's a present for you, Jack – he's all yours – if you want him, that is.'

Jack had turned quite pale, his eyes popping in surprise. He turned to Sally who was just behind him, her hands over her mouth, stifling a laugh, but her eyes dancing.

'Mine? Are you sure he's mine?' he stuttered. Then he squealed: 'Of course I want him! He's lovely! And Sally can help with him too, can't she?' he added, in an unexpected moment of generosity.

'We'll all help,' his Mum said, 'but he's your special responsibility now. When he's housetrained, he can sleep up in your bedroom – if he's not too naughty, that is!'

'Let's put the box down, in a warm corner, shall we, and let him explore the kitchen,' said Dad, and very gently, he lifted the little brown bundle onto Jack's lap. There the little pup lay, wriggling a little and yawning, while Mrs Bennett fetched a saucer with a few spoonfuls of dinner for him.

Bedtime was rather late that night. The puppy tottered round the kitchen, sniffing everything and leaving several small puddles on the floor, before settling back in his box and falling fast asleep.

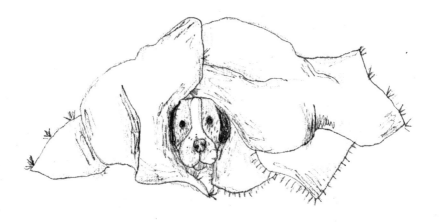

It turned out that Sally had been in on the secret but had sworn not to let on. She was to get a new dress as a present later, to soothe any jealousy. And there was certainly plenty of work now for all the family.

Chapter 9

The next day was Saturday; it was usually a morning for lying in late, but Jack and Sally were both up early to see the puppy.

Mrs Bennett was in the kitchen and Mr Bennett had left already to open up the shop. The puppy had just eaten some biscuits softened in a bit of gravy, and was now lapping at his water bowl, his little black ears flopping down.

Mrs Bennett told Jack how they had found the pup through the local vet.

'He was the runt of the litter,' she explained. 'That means he was the smallest pup – he had rather a lot of brothers and sisters, you know, and his mum wasn't managing to feed them all very well – she was a Jack Russell, so only a wee thing. So he had to have extra bottles of milk to keep him going – or else he might have died.'

Jack picked the puppy up gently and lifted him to his shoulder, where he snuggled up to lick Jack's ear.

'Here, take this old towel, and put it under him. He's going to take some time to house-train – we don't want all your clothes ruined before then!' Mum laughed. 'I've already done quite a lot of mopping this morning! But he shouldn't take long to train, I hope. Now, have you thought of a name for him?'

Jack shook his head, but by the end of the day, he announced that the puppy's name was to be Magic, because he was always disappearing – often all that could be seen was a little black nose poking from under the furniture. And everyone agreed it was the perfect name, so Magic it was.

The next few weeks were busy ones, especially for Mrs Bennett who only grumbled a bit about all the extra work the puppy gave her. There was a stream of visitors to the house: curious neighbours, the twins from Jack's class and Marian too, who dropped by on the Monday morning and was surprised to be greeted by high-pitched yapping when she rang the doorbell.

Peggy had heard of the Bennett's plans, of course, over cups of tea in the café. She had wondered if it wouldn't prove a lot of hard work for Mrs Bennett. But Mrs Bennett herself wasn't worried – she knew her husband had lived with dogs as a child at the family shop in Drayton. And when Peggy visited, she could see that all was going well.

'So how's Jack now?' she asked, while she rubbed Magic's chin as he stretched up on her knee, then pushing him off as he naughtily tried to pull her gloves from her pocket.

'You know, he's quite a changed boy!' Mrs Bennett said. 'From the moment Magic arrived, actually – he's been smiling again, thank goodness!'

'Worth all the extra work, then!' said Peggy. 'And Magic must make you smile too – he's a cheeky little chap, isn't he?'

The Bennetts soon got Magic's housetraining sorted, with lots of newspaper, and quick dashes to the front garden. Then Magic was allowed upstairs and his cosy new basket was moved up to Jack's bedroom.

The two parents poked their heads round Jack's door that night. Magic was not in his basket, but stretched out on the bed with his nose on Jack's shoulder.

'Not very hygienic,' whispered Mrs Bennett to her husband.

And he replied: 'But they do look happy, don't they?'

Chapter 10

The next few weeks flew by. The whole family had to keep alert for Magic's pranks. He chewed the edge of the stair-carpet; he brought in sticks and stones from the garden, and stole Jack's socks and turned them to shreds with his needle-sharp baby teeth. He would jump up onto a chair and steal a biscuit or a slice of bread from the table, if one was left carelessly within his reach. Sally got very good at remembering to keep her door firmly shut. And sometimes, even Jack lost his temper and shouted at Magic, chasing him round the house to rescue his school pencil-case from being torn to pieces.

'He's got a good nose, that dog!' Granddad would say when he visited. 'And with those ears, I shouldn't wonder if he's got some spaniel in him!'

But Magic kept them laughing most of the time, with his little tail wagging like a windscreen-wiper. And each night he leapt onto Jack's bed and stuck his nose into the blankets, his two back legs splayed out like a frog.

Miss Simms commented to Mrs Bennett that Jack was a lot brighter in class.

'Jack's been writing about Magic, you know, and I even persuaded him to read out his piece to the class. He told them that Magic talks to him at night. They've hatched a plan together, to find Charlie, he says. It's a sweet idea, don't you think?'

The Easter holidays began and suddenly all the daffodils were out. Mr Bennett was spending the lighter evenings digging his vegetable patch in the garden. Magic was proving a bit of a trial for him, showing a great fondness for digging holes in his newly worked beds, and in the lawn as well.

'I'll have to start again!' he complained, when his little bean plants, carefully nurtured for weeks in his greenhouse, were uprooted by an enthusiastic Magic.

'Or maybe leave them till next year,' Mrs Bennett, sympathetically patting him on the shoulder. 'He'll be a bit more sensible when he's older, I hope!'

'Maybe he'll have dug to Australia by then,' chipped in Sally, ruefully looking at the little piles of earth on the lawn, where Magic had excavated.

Mrs Bennett laughed: 'Oh dear, we wouldn't want to lose him down a hole, would we?' She turned to Mr Bennett: 'Perhaps a bit of chicken wire over the beans would stop his digging?'

So the vegetable patch became decorated with chicken wire borrowed from Granddad's garden shed, and upturned flower-pots sat over the many little holes in the lawn. This wasn't perfect but was enough to deter Magic from enlarging them each time he ventured into the back garden.

Chapter 11

One evening, Mr Bennett came back from work in a bad temper.

'I've lost the keys to the shop,' he complained as soon as he came in. 'When I got to work this morning, they weren't in my pocket – I had to wait for Nicos to arrive, and it was almost opening time before he turned up.' He sighed: 'Always a little bit late, that boy…I sent him out to hunt for the keys in case I had dropped them on the way – but no luck!'

'Perhaps you left them here?' replied Mrs Bennett, 'though I'm sure I'd have spotted them, if they were anywhere obvious. We'll have to do a thorough search.'

'It'll cost a packet if I have to get the locks changed – I can't risk having them fall into the wrong hands, and getting burgled! Maybe the dratted dog has picked them up – he'd think they were a good toy, I guess.'

'Well if he has, we'll find them somewhere,' said Mrs Bennett, in her usual reassuring way. 'And if not, we'd better call the police station to see if they've been handed in.'

So they began a hunt for the keys, and a reluctant Jack and Sally were roped in to help. They shook out cushions, and brushed out the sofa and looked under all the chairs, as well as in Magic's basket. They found a heap of oddments: coins, broken biscuits, combs and pencils, but no keys. And Magic lay with his head between his paws, quietly watching, lifting an eyebrow from time to time, as if trying to make sense of all this unusual activity. He was certainly going to miss his usual evening walk with Mr Bennett.

The next day was Saturday, and was Sally's turn to walk Magic. Mrs Bennett had started a strict rota for him, and all the family took their turn. Rain or shine, Magic needed his walks, even if, in the rain, they were sometimes very short.

Sally had not quite mastered the trick of getting the puppy to sit still while she hooked the lead onto his collar. Magic was leaping up and down and barking frantically in excitement.

' Silly dog!' she shouted, then wailed: 'Mum – can you help? He just won't sit still for me.'

Jack put his head round the door. He stood for a moment, shaking his head.

'Want me to do it?' he asked.

Sally looked like thunder for a moment. Then, saying nothing, she handed the lead to Jack. Jack stood for a moment with the lead behind his back. Magic soon sat down, and, in a trice, Jack slipped the lead on. It all looked so easy!

Mrs Bennett was watching from the kitchen doorway.

'It's hard at first, Sal. But if you stand still, he'll have to quieten, or he gets no walk!' she said.

And off Sally went with Magic, both going at a good lick.

Mrs Bennett went back to the kitchen to finish the washing up, and to make a cup of tea. It only seemed as if a moment had passed, when she heard Sally's voice, shrill with excitement at the front door.

'Mum, Jack, come and look!' she yelled. 'Magic's found Dad's keys!' And there they were, glinting in her outstretched hand.

'Goodness me!' said Mrs Bennett. 'How on earth did he do that?'

'Well, it was round the corner…we were just walking along, and then Magic suddenly just stopped – I couldn't get him to budge an inch. Then he started whining and jumping up at the wall, and there they were, on the top of the wall. Someone must have picked them up and put them there – I'd never have spotted them without Magic, they were pretty invisible.'

'Well, Dad will be relieved!' Mrs Bennett replied. 'And we should give Magic a treat for being so clever!'

But Magic was already getting his reward, a big hug and a romp on the floor with Jack.

'I gave him the right name, didn't I? See, he's special, isn't he?' Jack said, with his arms around Magic.

'Yes, we'll definitely agree on that,' said his Mum with a smile, as she bent down to scratch Magic under his chin.

Chapter 12

Jack's visit to Auntie May's in London had been arranged before Magic arrived in the Bennett household. It had been fixed for the summer half-term. The nearer it came, the more fidgety Jack became. What would he do without Magic's company, and for nearly a week too? They had plans, he solemnly explained to his Mum, to track down Charlie's whereabouts. Charlie had left his pyjamas in Jack's bedroom, for his occasional sleepovers. Jack was certain Magic could follow his scent from them.

'How would that be possible?' she had asked gently, explaining that the pyjamas had been washed since Charlie left. Jack was very upset. He buried his head under his pillow. What a stupid, idiotic thing to do!

Then Jack sat up. 'But there are still Charlie's slippers in the cupboard – Magic could use those,' he argued.

Mrs Bennett didn't reply. What could she say? She knew that no-one had heard from Charlie or his Mum for months now. And they might be anywhere.

Jack went into a sulk about the visit to London for a good few days, but gradually as the time grew near, he gave up his protest; he could see that his Mum and Dad were not going to let him off.

'We can't change the plans now,' Mrs Bennett had said. 'And besides, we'll take special care of Magic, don't you worry! And Auntie May has lots of treats planned for you – the Zoo, the Tower, the museum with dinosaur bones… You've always wanted to see that one, haven't you?'

So when the half-term holiday came, Mrs Bennett helped Jack to pack his suitcase and he and his Dad took the train to London. Mum, Sally and Magic came to the station to wave them off. Auntie May was to meet them at Paddington, and take Jack to Kentish Town by tube.

Auntie May had lived on her own since her husband had died, in a little flat off the Kentish Town Road. She had two cats, Dad had explained, and this was why Magic couldn't come too. Even Jack realised that Magic might come off worst in a scrap with any cat.

Auntie May's flat was in a row of tall Victorian buildings. There were dark stairs leading upwards, with polished wooden bannisters, lit only by a dim light bulb. But once in the flat, it was light and airy. There were high ceilings and the windows were wide, with lacy curtains draped in front of them. If Jack pulled these back, he could sit in the window and look down on the people and traffic scurrying below – red double-decker buses, lorries and cars, far busier than the view from his Abingdon house.

Auntie May was Nan's sister and looked quite like her – a bit taller but with white wavy hair. Jack had met her often, especially since Uncle Jim had died, because she came every Christmas to stay with Nan and Granddad. So he knew her well, but had never visited her flat before.

After Jack had unpacked in his tiny bedroom, Auntie May cooked supper. It was Jack's favourite beans-on-toast for supper, eaten in the kitchen at an old scrubbed oak table. Afterwards, Auntie May gave Jack a glass of milk and a plate of biscuits, and settled with a sigh into her easy chair in the living room.

'I thought we might go and see Buckingham Palace and perhaps have a boat trip on the Thames tomorrow. The weather forecast says it's set to be fine so we shouldn't miss the chance – it may not stay that way,' she said.

Jack said nothing, but nodded, his mouth full of biscuit. There was a pause:

'And I expect you'd like to phone home tonight. Your Mum tells me you might be worried about that little dog of yours!'

So Jack phoned home: 'Is Magic all right?' he asked. His Mum laughed.

'He's out for a walk with Dad just now. And he's eaten his dinner with his usual enthusiasm. But,' she added, 'he did spend most of the afternoon lying by the front door, as if he expected you to walk in at any moment.'

'Tell him I miss him, won't you?' Jack said, his throat suddenly feeling a bit tight as he put the phone down.

Chapter 13

The next day was as sunny and warm as the weather forecast had promised. Jack woke up in his attic bedroom, with bright checked curtains moving slightly in the breeze from an open window. He was missing Magic, but all the excitements of travelling had meant that he had fallen asleep quickly. Now he jumped out of bed and ran out into the hall. He could hear Auntie May, already up and about in the kitchen. There was a lovely smell of bacon and eggs wafting up, making Jack feel extremely peckish. He didn't dawdle and in a few minutes was downstairs, with a plateful of breakfast in front of him.

The visit to see Buckingham Palace went well, and Jack admired the guards in their bearskin hats and smartly polished boots. The river trip was fun too, especially as Auntie May bought him a portion of chips as a treat for him on the journey. They saw Tower Bridge and the Houses of Parliament, and when the boat docked again, Auntie May bought some postcards, reminding him he should send one to his parents, and to Sally as well.

'And Magic too.' Jack had added.

Jack wrote the postcards that evening, after supper, while Auntie May put her feet up after the busy day. The two cats huddled comfortably together, purring on her knee. Jack didn't dare to ask her how to spell 'parliament', so he just guessed at that. But he put lots of kisses on the one he sent to Magic, even though he knew he would demolish the card in seconds – Magic's favourite occupation was chewing up cardboard.

The rest of Jack's stay passed very quickly. He became quite confident at getting about on the Underground.

Auntie May had given him a map of the tube, so he could work out how to criss-cross London to see all the sights that she had planned. He became very used to jumping on and off the escalators, scary at first try, as well as enduring the noise and the crowds at the end of the day. On his last day, they took the bus to the Zoo. There they saw tigers and monkeys, elephants and snakes, as well as Jack's favorite, the penguins at feeding time, ducking and diving in their lovely white-painted pool.

Even with all this excitement, Jack was missing Magic badly – he had had enough of sight-seeing. Tomorrow, he'd be home.

Chapter 14

Jack had phoned home again, halfway through his stay. Was Magic OK? Yes, Magic was fine, Dad said, but he was obviously missing Jack: sitting with his head on his paws, staring at the front door.

But the next day, something awful happened, that turned the day upside-down. It was mid-morning, and Mrs Bennett heard the front door bang. Someone had left it on the latch and it was swinging in the wind. When she went to click the latch to shut it, she noticed the front gate was open too. And where was Magic? He was nowhere to be seen, nor was he in the back garden, where he often spent time snooping around looking for sticks or stones to chew.

It was obvious Magic had slipped out.

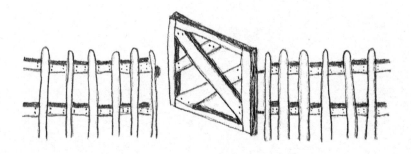

In a panic, Mrs Bennett yelled to Sally, and she came rushing down the stairs, closely followed by her friend Marcie, who had just dropped in for a chat. Together they spent some time calling in the garden and up the stairs, and then out in the road. There was absolutely no sight nor sound of Magic.

It was Sally's quick decision to go straight out and search the nearby roads.

'We'll be back in ten minutes!' Sally shouted to her Mum, over her shoulder. 'But you stay here, just in case he comes back on his own.'

Then off they rushed down the road. Both were long-legged girls, and they raced off, Marcie going one way, and Sally the other. Mrs Bennett could hear them calling Magic's name long after they had disappeared from view.

Mrs Bennett sat down rather suddenly – she was surprised to find her legs shaking like jelly under her. All sorts of terrors rushed through her mind – what if Magic had got run over, or stuck somewhere, or fell in the river. Jack would never forgive them…

Her first thought was to call Mr Bennett at the shop. Nicos answered – he was working extra hours that week, clearing out the clutter in the little storeroom the back of the shop. He picked up from Mrs Bennett's strained voice that something was wrong, and rushed immediately to fetch her husband.

'Eddie, it's Magic – he's run off, we can't find him…' Mrs Bennett gave a sob, and she had to fumble in her pocket for a hankie.

Now it was her husband's turn to be a comforter:

'Don't worry, love,' he said. 'He knows his way round the neighbourhood by now. And he's very friendly, someone will pick him up – he's only a little 'un, and he's got his address tag on his collar, hasn't he?' He could hear the sobs getting quieter on the end of the line.

'Why don't you call the police station, and ask the dog warden if he's been spotted anywhere? The more eyes on the look-out the better. And let me know if you find him! I can't leave the shop now, but I'll get some fish-and-chips for us all on the way home – you won't want to be cooking tonight.'

Sally and Marcie came in a few minutes later. They were quite subdued – there was no trace of Magic. Sally gave her mother a questioning look, but said nothing; Mum crying must be bad. Marcie suggested pinning up 'lost dog' notices on nearby streets, so the two girls got to work with paper and bold coloured pens. It took nearly all morning, and then they were off again, taking with them some strong tape to fix the posters up. Meanwhile, Mrs Bennett spent some time on the phone, to the Abingdon police and to the dog warden. They were sympathetic and said they would keep on the lookout, and would ring back if they heard anything.

After lunch, Mrs Bennett felt suddenly very tired, and almost fell asleep in her chair with her cup of tea. Marcie had gone home, leaving Sally restlessly pacing up and down. Usually in the holidays, she'd be up in her room listening to her favourite pop music; now she couldn't settle to anything. After an hour of waiting, she couldn't bear it any longer. She went out to hunt the streets again – this time taking a lead in her pocket.

It was going to be a long day.

Chapter 15

It was late afternoon, and Sally was back again, empty-handed. She and her Mum were in the kitchen when the doorbell rang. The two of them jumped in fright – they were both so on edge with worry. Sally rushed to the front door. A young man stood in the porch. She could see at once that he was holding a wriggling Magic in his arms.

'I'm sorry, I did try to phone, but I thought it was better to come straight here…' he began, but he was drowned out with the whoop of delight from Sally who leapt forward to scoop the little dog up in her arms. The young man staggered backwards slightly, and Magic slid out of his arms and into Sally's.

'Oops!' he cried, as he regained his footing, adding: 'Well, I've obviously come to the right place!'

Mrs Bennett, who was just behind Sally, was quite overcome, and for a moment was at a loss for words.

'Please come in!' she stammered at last, 'And where on earth did you find him?'

The young man was in uniform, his peaked cap now tilted at a crazy angle.

'That's very kind, thank you,' he explained, 'but I can't stay long. I'm meant to be on duty at the station, and I have to get back. That's where we found him this afternoon.'

Sally and her Mum looked at each other.

' The station! How on earth did he get there?' Mrs Bennett cried. 'It's over a mile away!'

The young man shrugged – he only knew what he'd seen, he said. Then Mrs Bennett insisted he come in, completely ignoring his protestations that he had to hurry back. She rushed to the kitchen and made a pot of tea. When a large slice of ginger cake mysteriously appeared on the tea-tray, he was finally persuaded to sit down and tuck in. Mrs Bennett and Sally peppered him with questions: how, where, what and when all tumbled out in quick succession.

The young man, who was called Bernard, tried to help them piece the story together. Magic had been spotted on the station platform, about lunchtime, he said – sitting quite quiet and still. One of the passengers had asked Bernard if the dog was his, as he wasn't on a lead and he didn't seem to be with anyone.

'I hadn't noticed him until then, but we took him into the office and gave him a bowl of water – he was pretty thirsty. We saw his tag of course, and I managed to tie a piece of string to his collar. Then I volunteered to take him here in the back of my car – I love dogs and I was pretty sure he'd be no trouble. He's a friendly little thing, isn't he?'

The first thing that Mrs Bennett did, after Bernard had driven off back to the station, was to phone the shop to tell her husband.

When Mr Bennett arrived home at last, it was with a large hot parcel of fish and chips in his hands, as he had promised. The three of them sat round the kitchen table, feasting on the juicy fish and chips, and Magic got a share of fish too, when they had eaten all they could.

'I do wonder if Magic wasn't waiting for Jack at the station,' said Mr Bennett thoughtfully. 'Could he have missed him so much that he went looking where he last saw Jack?'

'We'll never know, will we?' Mrs Bennett replied, 'but it does seem he's got an uncanny knack of finding his way...'

'Do you think he knew Jack was coming home soon?' chipped in Sally, who was beginning to believe what Jack always said, that there was something unusual about Magic. 'Maybe he will help Jack find Charlie, after all?'

'Well, that's a fanciful idea, isn't it?' said Mrs Bennett. 'And before you all get carried away, you can give a hand with the plates – not much washing-up, but it must be done!'

' And tomorrow we'll be fetching Jack from the station again,' said Mr Bennett, adding, with a frown: 'What *would* we have said if Magic was still lost? It doesn't bear thinking about! We need to keep that gate shut – I'd better fix it to make sure it doesn't swing open like that again!'

'Well, I'll be taking the station people a bunch of flowers from the garden,' said Mrs Bennett with emphasis. 'It's the least we can do. They deserve huge thanks from us, don't they?'

And rather tired out from the day's excitement, they all decided – even Sally – on an early bed-time.

Chapter 16

The next morning, Mrs Bennett was brushing her hair, sitting on the edge of the bed.

' Just what are we going to tell Jack today?' she asked Mr Bennett. 'Seriously, it's a big problem isn't it? Perhaps just not mention it? He won't be pleased if he gets to hear of it, will he?'

'Mmm, you're right, we need to agree what we say, don't we? Can we try and play it down, at least…?' her husband replied thoughtfully.

'I think we should say nothing – it'll only upset him,' Mrs Bennett replied.

So that was the plan.

Later that morning, they set off for the station with a large bunch of flowers, including a thank-you note for Bernard. Magic was made a great fuss of, playing the star, his eyes closing with an expression of bliss when he was stroked and patted.

'Please don't tell Jack when he arrives!' Mrs Bennett begged everyone. 'We don't want him upset...'

Jack was making the return journey on his own. Auntie May had put him on the train at Paddington, telling him he was to look out for his parents waiting on the platform when he arrived at Radley Station. Otherwise, she warned, he would sail on to Oxford, and that would cause problems – it would take ages longer to find him. So Jack was anxiously peering out of the rather murky train windows, well before the train slowed into the station.

Magic was quiet until he spotted Jack, and then started to dance about on the end of his lead, squealing loudly. Jack dropped his suitcase and rushed with arms outstretched. How he had missed him! His eyes were stinging with tears as Magic leapt up, climbing right on to his shoulder, with a noise that sounded almost as if he was singing with joy.

'Both happy now!' Mr Bennett laughed, as he retrieved Jack's suitcase and they all turned to head for home.

Jack might have stayed in the dark about Magic's escapade. But Sally had forgotten to take all the 'lost dog' notices down, and when Jack spotted one stuck to a tree, there was some explaining to do.

Jack went into a fury after he'd winkled the story out of Sally. He rushed to his room and the door slammed with a spectacular bang. Sally's mouth fell open: she had never seen Jack in such a rage.

'Stupid, stupid people – he might have got run over! He might have been killed!' A guilty silence fell on the house, broken only by Jack's sobs from behind the closed door.

'Leave him a bit,' said Mrs Bennett. 'Magic will calm him down, just you see.'

And Magic did. When all was quiet again, Mrs Bennett went in and found Jack and Magic both asleep amongst the crumpled sheets and blankets. She covered them both over with a quilt, and pulling the curtains to, tiptoed out.

The next morning, Mr Bennett showed Jack the cunning weight on a string that he'd fixed to the gate – Granddad's idea, he said, which meant the gate always swung closed as you came through.

Chapter 17

Jack didn't often talk about Charlie now, but he often looked at a small photo of himself and Charlie taken last Christmas, which Mrs Bennett had prised out of the family photo album. And every night before bed, he opened the cupboard in his bedroom, and solemnly showed Magic the pair of slippers left by Charlie when he used to stay over, when Mrs Munroe worked nights at the hospital. Magic always gave them a good sniff,

 and Jack would whisper into Magic's floppy ear that the slippers were Charlie's, and when the time was right, they'd go on a hunt for him.

So when the plans for the summer holidays

came up in conversation one tea-time, Jack blurted out that he wanted to hunt for Charlie in the holidays.

'I'm taking Charlie's slippers with me, wherever we go,' he announced very firmly. 'Magic can use them to find him then…if he's nearby, of course.'

No-one wanted to pour cold water on this plan, though the other three round the table all thought it was a mad-cap notion. There was a silence for a moment. Then Mrs Bennett said:

'We were thinking of going to Cornwall for a couple of weeks this summer. You know Uncle Bill lives in Penzance. Well, they've offered to let us use their house – they're off to France this August. What do you kids think of that idea?'

There was a shriek of delight from both Jack and Sally – it was brilliant!

'Mind you, there'll be a good deal of travelling to get there – it's a long way!' Mr Bennett added.

'And Magic can come too?' Jack asked, with a hint of anxiety in his voice. He couldn't think of leaving Magic again.

When he heard the answer 'yes', Jack's face burst into a smile that lasted the rest of the day. So it was all agreed.

Chapter 18

It was only a few weeks till the summer holidays began; they would set off to Penzance a week after that. Jack fretted: how could he wait that long! But the time flew by, what with sorting out what was to be taken, packing and working how it would all fit in to the car. Mr Bennett was splashing out and hiring a car for the holiday – the van wouldn't be any use, Mr Bennett said, as it only had two seats at the front.

Jack was given a suitcase to fill, which he stuffed very quickly, with everything higgledy-piggledy. Mrs Bennett took one look at the pile of crumpled clothes, and sighed. She emptied it out and showed Jack how much more you could get in if it was all neatly folded. At the bottom of the case, she found Charlie's slippers.

One look at Jack's face as she lifted them out, made her put them carefully back. Then she started to repack, saying nothing. Jack was clearly intent on trying to find Charlie, and she knew no amount of arguing about it would change his mind.

At last the big day arrived. Mrs Bennett woke the children very early – they were to set off at four in the morning to avoid the traffic. It was going to be a very long drive. Jack and Sally were only half awake, bleary-eyed as they sat at the kitchen table, pecking at jam buns and sipping a glass of milk each. Meanwhile their parents tried to fit all the holiday stuff, now piled up in the hall, into the car. Magic was unusually subdued, lying in his basket with a worried look on his face.

Magic's basket was the last thing to be squeezed into the car boot – thankfully it fitted, and they were ready to go. So off they set, the early morning light throwing a pink glow on little puffs of cloud in the pale blue sky.

Jack and Sally hadn't shaken off their morning drowsiness and almost immediately fell asleep, their heads lolling against the windows. But Magic was transfixed and very wide-awake; he stuck his nose up to the window, which was open

a crack, and half-closed his eyes, drinking in all the new sights and smells of the journey.

The journey was a slow one, broken from time to time with a stop for Magic to drink and stretch his legs, and for a sip from the thermos flask of cool lemonade for everyone else. As they approached the West Country, the traffic thickened and slowed to a crawl. They had a quick picnic in the car park of Stonehenge – hard-boiled eggs, ham sandwiches and an apple. The sun was hot now, and both the parents had a quick snooze, their car seats pushed back, and a rolled-up coat in place of a pillow. Jack and Sally meanwhile, took Magic for a brisk walk down a grassy slope next to the car park, with the huge ancient stones visible in the distance and with the sound of bees humming in the clover.

Off they set again, Sally in the back with an adventure story on her knee, and Jack hugging Magic, both feeling better for the walk, but already sick of the travelling, and beginning to feel very bored.

On and on they crept, with the traffic slow all the way. Both Jack and Magic fell asleep again and even Sally shut her book and dozed off. A cry from Mrs Bennett woke them suddenly – she had spotted a thin glittering line of gold between two hills.

'It's the sea!' she shouted in delight. Jack and Sally bounced up from their seats – surely they were nearly there now!

'Not long from here,' said Mr Bennett, with a grin. 'We're on the outskirts of Penzance!'

And so at long last the journey was over, and they were all tumbling out of the car, stretching stiff limbs and yawning, with Magic leaping about in his usual wild manner. Mrs Bennett unlocked the door to Uncle Bill's house and they all rushed in.

A note on the table from Uncle Bill and Auntie Kathleen told them there was supper in the fridge – soup and pasties, and a special treat of apple pie with clotted cream as well. They had left the night before, for their holiday in France, but had thoughtfully left their visitors a welcome feast after their long journey.

Chapter 19

Jack woke early the next morning, sitting up slowly and rubbing his eyes. Magic was curled up at the end of the bed, but he was soon stretching and leaping off, eager to go outside. Jack knew he had to let him out quickly. He dressed in a hurry and ran down the stairs. Sally was sitting at the kitchen table already, with a bowl of cereal in front of her and another adventure story in her hand.

Jack opened the front door and let Magic out, while he searched for some dog biscuits for Magic's breakfast. Sally dropped her book and put her head out of the front door.

She took a deep breath of the lovely clear air. The sun was out and the little street was empty – it must still be quite early, she thought. She turned to Jack.

'Let's explore!' Jack nodded, and so they grabbed a lead for Magic and set off at once, without a thought, walking down the lane to the main road, heading for where they hoped they would find the beach. Magic's nose was to the ground and his tail wagging with excitement.

It wasn't long before they reached the sea-front. There, ahead of them, was the famous seawater swimming pool. Jack had heard about this from his parents. Just try it, his Mum had said – you'll find it's really freezing! Jack and Sally looked over the edge of the pool. The water was clear, but the pool-sides were covered with hundreds of sea-snails clustered thickly together. Ugh, Jack thought, I'm not going in there!

They walked on a little further to see the little boats bobbing in the harbour, the sea sparkling in the early morning sunshine. Jack was beginning to feel hungry – he'd had no breakfast yet. So he and Sally turned back, tugging on Magic's lead to set off for home. It was at the main road crossing that it dawned on them both that they didn't know Uncle Bill's address.

'Oh no, which way home?' Sally cried, 'was it left or right here?'

They stood for a moment, dumbfounded.

'And the address?' Sally added, looking at Jack in the faint hope that he would remember it. Jack shook his head – it all looked so different now. The traffic had now started to build up. Cars were whizzing past them, creating quite a breeze.

Sally groaned: 'Oh, what idiots we are! How on earth will we find the way?' They were silent for a moment, then Jack said in a quiet voice:

'We'll just have to trust Magic.' Jack turned and took the lead from Sally.

'Some hope!' she said. But Jack was already bending down low over Magic's head. He rubbed his ears gently, and murmured softly. To Jack's surprise, Sally didn't argue; her usual bossiness seemed to have vanished into thin air.

In a break in the traffic, they set off, Jack holding the lead quite loose. Magic, eager as ever, rushed straight over the main road and then turned into the maze of little streets that they had come through. It seemed a miracle, but soon Jack and Sally could see the red door of Uncle Bill's house just ahead of them.

'Don't tell that we got lost,' Sally whispered. 'We'll be in trouble. And they'll only worry, won't they?'

Jack nodded, and put his finger to his lips: 'No, we won't tell.'

They rang the doorbell and Mrs Bennett opened the door:

'Gracious, where have you two been?' she asked as she let them in. 'We were wondering if we should send out a search party! But you're just in time – breakfast's on the table!'

Chapter 20

Jack now took Magic on an early walk most days. But he made sure to check his route carefully as he and Magic went along – he'd learned a lot from the fright on that first day. Soon he was easily finding his way down to the harbour. It was the way that Magic always wanted to go, and pulled harder on the lead the nearer they got. Why was it, thought Jack, that every morning they ended up in the same place, leaning on the white-painted barricade, looking out at the boats bobbing on the tide. One morning, an old man joined them, puffing on a pipe and humming a little tune between puffs.

'That'll be the Scilly ship coming in,' he said, turning towards Jack. 'It'll have been a rough crossing – there's been quite a breeze this morning.'

Jack said nothing – it didn't make sense. How could a ship be silly, he wondered. There was a moment's silence, then the old man asked:

'Does your dog like fish? Looks like he'd fancy a taste of those fresh pilchards down on the quay, I reckon.'

And indeed Magic was pulling on the lead in the direction of some steep steps, scrabbling at the stones set in the harbour wall that led steeply downwards. Below him, Jack could see the crowded quayside. There were indeed plenty of boxes stacked up on carts, full to overflowing with fish, glinting in the sun. Lots of people were rushing about, and there was a huge hubbub of shouting.

In the harbour, there were little boats and big boats, tied up hugger-mugger, with the 'silly ship' coming into its own berth, a distance away, but still towering above them. It looked quite scary to Jack. Magic was still pulling on the lead. Suddenly in a flash, Jack understood. It was the signal he'd been waiting for! Here and now! His brain was in a whirl. Magic was telling him it was time to start the hunt for Charlie!

Would he be in trouble if he went onto the quayside? He didn't know – but his mouth turned dry with fear. And excitement too. But he wasn't ready – it was all too sudden. Tomorrow he'd come down again – this time, ready to go wherever Magic would take him.

Later that morning, the Bennett family set off in the car for a small seaside village near Penzance. A picnic was packed, bucket and spades, swimwear and towels piled into the car. They'd had lovely weather in the days after their arrival. And today was another perfect day for the beach. But Jack wasn't in the mood. He was thinking, sitting so quiet that his parents became quite worried. At lunch-time, he sat silently munching his sandwiches.

'What's bitten you, Jack?' his Mum asked. 'Are you feeling all right?'

Jack sighed, and gave a rather damp and sandy Magic a hug. Sally had given up trying to persuade Jack to build a giant castle with her. She walked off in a huff, to poke about in the rock pools for shrimps and crabs. Magic at least was having a whale of a time, digging holes in the sand and rushing in and out of the little waves lapping the shore, not daring to venture in deep, but barking furiously. Jack watched him and slowly began to cheer up. It was rather hard not to smile while watching Magic's antics. And now Jack had a plan for tomorrow in his head.

Chapter 21

Jack hardly slept that night. He tiptoed about his room after bedtime, packing his duffle bag for the adventure tomorrow. He had taken his purse of saved-up pocket money – nearly a pound in loose change. He had filled a bottle with water, twisting the cap tightly so it wouldn't leak. He knew Magic would get thirsty. He had stuffed a handful of dog biscuits in a paper bag into the pocket of his shorts, with a few surreptitiously stolen biscuits for himself too. And most important of all, he had taken Charlie's slippers and had given Magic a good sniff of them.

'Tomorrow we're going to find Charlie!' he had whispered into Magic's ear, before wedging the slippers carefully into the bottom of the duffle bag.

When he woke, there was a glow of pale light behind the curtains. Jack checked his watch – it was five-thirty. Brilliant, he thought – he was sure no-one in the house would be awake yet. He dressed in a hurry, grabbed his bag, and crept downstairs, carrying a rather surprised dog in his arms, trying to make no noise. Holding his breath, he took his jacket from the hook, and spotted Magic's lead – he'd need that! He stood for a moment in front of the door, his heart beating fast. Then quickly he turned the latch, pushed the door and closed it quietly behind him. Tip-toeing down the steps, he slung his bag over his shoulder, and fixed Magic's lead. He was ready at last: there was no going back now!

The route to the harbour was familiar by now, so the two of them set off at a cracking pace, and soon the little huddle of boats came into view. The tide was not fully in, and there were only a few people around, working on their boats, scrubbing and polishing and waiting for the tide.

Jack and Magic found a bench, and sat down. Jack fished around and gave Magic one of his biscuits, and pulled out a sweet one he saved for himself. He felt suddenly famished, and realised the biscuits were going to have to do as breakfast, and perhaps lunch as well. Lucky he had his pocket money, Jack thought, but even that wouldn't go far.

Jack was in a bit of a dream now, gazing over the harbour. But Magic wasn't going to let him rest – tugging at the lead, fussing at Jack's knee.

'O.K, let's go!' said Jack, jumping up at last. So off they went, Jack making no effort to rein Magic in. He was just going to let Magic follow his instincts. Soon they found themselves round the harbour wall and looking at the same boat the old man had called 'the silly ship'. People were clambering up the walkway onto the ship carrying suitcases, and on the quay, there was a queue of children waiting to board.

Magic wasted no time, but sat down firmly close to them. There was no doubt that here he meant to stay.

'Oh gosh,' Jack thought. ' I've got no ticket, and not enough money for one either!'

The queue of children started to move. Jack had a sudden idea – he picked Magic up and slid him bottom first into his duffle bag. There was just room. And Jack's anorak loosely folded on top made a perfect hiding place. Only Magic's little nose poked out from under the jacket. He stayed quite quiet and still, as Jack shuffled forward with the other children.

'All right, kids! Move along there', a loud voice shouted – someone in uniform and a peaked cap, waving a piece of paper, was pushing the children along the gangway. Jack's heart was pounding. Clutching his precious load, he kept his head down, moving along with the others. Would they let him on? Only when the children just ahead of him started running along the deck with shrieks of excitement, did Jack risk looking around. He was safely aboard – amazing, but somehow he'd done it!

Looking around cautiously, he put down his bag and tipped it forward, so Magic could crawl out. Magic shook himself, and lifted his nostrils to the wind. Suddenly, a huge foghorn sounded, booming out from the ship over the harbour.

There was smoke coming from a yellow funnel, and Jack was suddenly aware of a gentle vibration beneath his feet. They were setting sail! The open sea was ahead of them and the harbour fast sliding away into the distance.

The ship was quite a big one, Jack could see, now he was able to walk up and down. You could go below, where there were chairs, but Jack thought he'd be safer from awkward questions if he stayed on deck. It was a lovely morning, the sea a deep twinkling blue and not a cloud in the sky. Jack leant on the railings, with Magic beside him, breathing in the salt air, and watching the seagulls whirling and calling over the ship. Suddenly a voice next to him made him jump.

'I didn't see that you had a little dog with you! What's his name?'

It was a girl from the party of children he had come on board with. She'd been just in front of him in the queue. He remembered her from her ginger hair, tied back in a loose bunch, but almost long enough to sit on.

'He's called Magic.' he said, suddenly feeling a surge of alarm at the prospect of some difficult questions.

'I'm Rosemary,' she said. 'But everyone always calls me Rosie.'

'And I'm Jack'. There was a long pause. Jack didn't know what to say. But Rosie seemed eager to talk – and there was no escaping her now.

'I'm on a school trip to the Scilly Isles. We're camping on Tresco. Which island are you going to?'

Jack hadn't thought of a story for himself. A bit of quick thinking was needed, but his mind went blank.

' Er, er,' he stammered, desperately searching for a sensible answer. 'I'm going to stay with an auntie – she's meeting me off the boat…' Jack's inspiration dried up at this point. But it seemed enough for Rosie, and she didn't ask any more questions.

'She'll be on St Mary's, I expect,' she added, helpfully. 'We had to do a project about the Isles of Scilly, before this holiday, so I know all the names: St Mary's is the biggest island, though it's still tiny really. You can walk around it in a few hours.'

Jack suddenly relaxed, and smiled. Rosie couldn't know how much help she'd given him. He knew where he was headed now, and he had a story. Hopefully this would do to get him by. There was a moment of quiet, the two children watching the churning white foam of the ship's wake rushing past below them.

' I hope you don't get seasick,' Rosie said. 'The sea can be very rough on this crossing. We've all been given seasickness tablets to suck before we got on board.'

Jack said nothing. He'd never been on a boat at sea before. No point in worrying now – he'd have to wait and see. Meanwhile there was the ship to explore. So wrapping Magic's lead firmly round his wrist, he and Rosie set off round the upper deck, peering in to everything, counting the lifeboats, and then finding a bench out of the wind where they sat down. Magic jumped up onto Rosie's lap and stuck his nose into her hair. She squealed and wriggled with delight. Jack had some trouble getting Magic to quieten down. He didn't want to catch unwanted attention, while he was on board without a ticket.

Rosie was right about the crossing. Though the sun still shone, the sea got steadily rougher as time went by. Jack was glad he'd not had a proper breakfast. His stomach felt distinctly peculiar, and his head felt giddy. Rosie offered to get a drink from the cafeteria below. Jack nodded – his legs were beginning to feel like jelly.

'Just sit tight and look at the horizon,' Rosie advised. 'My dad says that helps sometimes. And take deep breaths too.' She reminded him of Sally for a moment – a bit bossy, but just now, Jack was grateful.

Rosie scuttled off to the cafeteria, and came back with two bottles of orange juice.

'Don't go down to the loos,' she said. 'There's an awful lot of people being sick already! Yuck, it's disgusting!'

Jack took the orange drink gratefully, and sipped it slowly. His stomach seemed to turn over each time the ship rolled – he couldn't remember ever feeling as bad as this. He shut his eyes, which seemed to help. Even Rosie had stopped chattering. They both sat in silence for what seemed like an eternity.

Suddenly Rosie jumped up and yelled:

'There's an island! Look, see, over there!' And indeed there was, a misty shape on the horizon. There were rocks too, high and sharp, rising out of the sea on either side of the boat, some with seals basking on them.

'We'll be in St Mary's in no time now!' Rosie declared confidently. And indeed, to Jack's great relief, they could see the little island coming quickly closer. Now the boat was turning, with a roar of its engines, till it bumped gently against the quay.

'I've got to go, or I'll be in trouble!' Rosie said, turning to pat Magic on the head. 'Have a good holiday!' And she shot off, her hair flying, to join her school group.

Jack's seasickness almost forgotten, he scooped Magic up and popped him once again in his bag, and followed slowly after her. She soon disappeared into the crowd that was waiting to disembark. There was a long wait but eventually, he was off the boat and standing on a long curved quay, with a high sea wall beside it, all built of huge blocks of stone. Most of the ship's passengers, carting suitcases, rucksacks and bags, were hurrying ahead off the quay towards a little town ahead. Magic, impatient as ever, was already tugging on his lead to follow them.

Chapter 22

It didn't take long for Jack and Magic to walk through the little town to reach a small grassy patch that overlooked the harbour. The Scilly ship could still be seen in the distance, but here were lots of tiny boats floating on the high tide, little waves smacking and slapping at their sides. Seagulls swooped and called plaintively overhead. Jack threw himself down on the grass, and lay soaking in the sunshine. He'd got quite chilly on the boat and was glad of the warmth. His stomach was beginning to recover from his seasickness, and he started to feel more than a little hungry. He'd not eaten anything other than a few biscuits all morning! There was an ice-cream van parked at the corner of the grass. There might be just enough of his pocket-money for an ice-cream perhaps? Soon he was licking a large one with a flake stuck in it. The van had a dog's water-bowl on the ground bedside it and Magic lapped at it, after Jack had emptied his pockets of the stash of dog-biscuits. They both lay on the grass contentedly.

Jack was almost asleep, when Magic nuzzled at his ear.

'OK, OK! We'll get going!' Jack scrambled to his feet again, rather reluctantly. He would have liked to rest for a while longer. He took Magic's lead with a sigh, and they set off. Magic led the way as always; Jack had no choice but to follow. Up the hill they went, past a lifeboat station at the edge of the harbour, Magic's nose to the ground, and his tail wagging.

The road led upwards and soon there were high hedges on each side, and walls of huge granite blocks. This led on to a narrow lane, deeply shaded on each side with overhanging bracken and ivy. They passed some large houses, all set far back from the road. Magic seemed confident, but Jack's spirits began to flag. There were bare fields on either side of the lane, and some strange-looking trees overhanging the road. It all looked rather gloomy, and there wasn't a soul about.

Jack suddenly noticed that it was turning chilly. A stiff breeze was blowing up that made the trees sigh. He looked up and, to his surprise, saw the sun was disappearing behind huge clouds, which had seemed to appear from nowhere. They looked black and threatening and were piled high in the sky. He took his jacket out of his duffle bag and slipped it on. The road went on and on, now up, now down, but Magic was as keen as ever, not letting Jack stop.

It wasn't long before the rain started: big drops at first, hissing as they hit the hot road. Then soon falling hard in sheets, grey and cold. Jack could feel the rain seeping through his jacket, wetting his hair and trickling down his neck. Magic was quickly becoming soaked, his fur sticking to his skin. He slowed down and started whimpering. His tail was between his legs, as they huddled beneath a tree for a moment or two. The blue sky had rapidly vanished, and Jack heard a grumble of thunder. Magic heard this too. Thunderstorms were the one thing that scared him. Jack could see he was shaking now and huddling close to Jack's feet. The rain fell harder than ever, coming down in cold torrents, so that even the tree gave them no protection. Flashes of lightning were coming every few moments, and the thunder was roaring. Jack was in despair now. With Magic in a fright, they'd never get anywhere. They were well and truly lost!

For the first time, Jack thought of home, how his mother would be worrying sick. He could see her face clearly now, all tearstained, Dad hugging her. How silly he'd been to think Magic could find a way to Charlie. It was just a mad idea. Hot tears mixed with the rain on his face, as he bent to pat Magic.

Suddenly Magic gave a yip. Was that a sound of a dog's bark in the distance? Yes, surely, a yapping noise, a bit louder now. And if there were dogs, there might be people. Putting his head down, Jack rushed from the shelter of the tree. Round a bend ahead, there were two dogs, black and white border collies, barking and jumping excitedly behind an old farm gate. Jack hesitated. They sounded quite aggressive. But as he came closer, he could see there was someone with them. Jack broke into a run.

'Well, I never! What have we got here?'

An elderly man wrapped in a grey mud-splattered raincoat was approaching the gate. There was a battered sign across it saying

'Tremaine Farm'. Jack opened his mouth, but no sound came. He was completely choked – not a word came out.

'Two drowned rats, by the look of it!' said the man. 'Well, come in now, and don't mind my dogs, they won't hurt ye.'

He pushed open the gate and grabbed Jack's arm and hurried him through the muddy yard, and into the farmhouse ahead, Magic scampering along with them. The three of them stood in the porch, dripping water onto the mat, all of them out of breath.

The old man shouted: 'Martha, I'll need a hand, a bit o' help – right now!'

'Just give me a minute, I'm covered in flour!' came the answering reply, a woman's voice this time. It wasn't long before she appeared, an elderly lady with grey, wavy hair, her red cheeks shiny from the heat of her kitchen. She wore an apron, and her arms were dusted with flour.

'Bless me, whatever's happened?' she cried. 'Bring 'em into the kitchen, Harry. By the fire – they look frozen.'

She stood for a moment, looking at the two wet creatures, water still dripping off the pair of them. 'I'll need towels, and one for the dog too.'

Harry stomped off, his big outdoor boots echoing up the stairs. It didn't take Martha long to wrap Jack up and rub some of the water out of his hair and his clothes. Then she turned to Magic, scooping him up in an old blanket and rubbing him firmly, before setting him down on the worn mat in front of the fire, where logs were burning merrily. The two of them sat, shivering still, but gratefully basking in the heat.

'It's my baking day,' Martha explained, 'So you chose the right moment! 'Spect you'd like a taste of my pie when it's done! Famous across the island, my pies are!' she added proudly. 'I hope you'll stay for a taste!'

Martha turned and went back to her pastry-making, rolling it out on a big wooden board, white with flour. Now Jack was feeling better, he looked around the kitchen. There were all sorts of crockery displayed on the walls, blue and white, patterned and striped. Kitchen implements hung higgledy-piggledy on a long rack along one wall. And there was a mouth-watering smell coming from a pan simmering on the kitchen stove.

She didn't seem in a hurry to ask questions, but went and fetched a cup of milk and some biscuits for Jack, and set down a bowl of dog biscuits and

some water for Magic. They were both famished –
they had been a long time without a proper meal.

Chapter 23

Harry came in and pulled his boots off, pouring a cup of tea from the large brown pot on the table. Only when they'd all finished, and with Magic already fast asleep on the hearth, did Martha ask tactfully: ' Have you come far?'

Jack covered his face with his hands, and found himself sobbing and gasping, and unable to answer. Martha stood up and put her arms round him, in a hug.

'Not to worry,' she said soothingly. 'Take your time, now.'

Jack took a deep breath, then after a few moments he began to explain. It all came out as rather a jumble. Martha listened patiently, bending close, with a frown of concentration on her face. It took some time before she made sense of what he was telling her. At last she grasped

that Jack's family were back in Penzance, and, worse still, certainly didn't know where he was. She turned quickly to Harry.

'Harry, we'll have to call the Hugh Town constable,' she said. 'We need to let the police know he's safe here.'

Harry sighed and went off to phone. It wasn't long before he was back.

'They've just called the Penzance police – there's a big search on for you, my lad. They're mightily relieved to hear you're safe. The constable's coming over here shortly, to see for himself.'

Jack's heart sank – now the police were after him. He started to cry again. Magic woke up and immediately jumped up and put his head in Jack's lap. Martha, who was now putting the finishing touches to the pastry on her pie, tutted and said:

'Don't worry, Jack! William won't bite – he's a softie, that's for sure, and he's got a boy about your age too.' She handed him a large handkerchief from her pocket, to wipe his nose.

They didn't have long to wait before they heard the growl of a motor scooter coming up to the farm gate. The policeman came in to a warm welcome from Martha. He was obviously well known.

'Good to see you, William' she said taking his wet coat and shaking it out onto the back of a chair. 'There's a fresh pot of tea just made, so do sit down! And here's the young lad they've all been looking for!'

William was a burly man with a round, red face, carrying a bike helmet in his hand. He said nothing as he sat down at the table, and gave a long hard look at Jack, as if he didn't know quite where to begin.

'We've told your parents that we've found you, Jack. They've been in quite a state. And we've said we'll try and get you back to them tonight.'

He paused and then asked gently: 'But perhaps you'd like to tell us why you ran away?'

Jack was sitting, head down, looking very shamefaced, still worrying that he was going to be arrested. But at this question, he jumped up.

'But I didn't run away!'

'Well, it looks like that to us – left home without telling anyone, not even a note…' the policeman continued quietly. 'You must have planned it for quite a time, getting on the boat to St Mary's, and all.'

Jack bit his lip. It would sound so silly now. What could he say?

Martha broke in: 'Just tell us why you did it, then. We do need to know.'

Jack lifted his head and said in a small voice: 'I was trying to find my friend. And Magic was going to help me, you see…'

His voice tailed away. How could he explain? They wouldn't understand.

'Ah, yes, your parents mentioned this. Would this be Charlie then?'

There was a long silence, broken only by sniffling from Jack. The policeman continued:

'But you haven't found him, have you? A bit of a wild goose chase after all, wasn't it?' The policeman leaned back in his chair, and frowned at Jack.

'Well, you're in for a treat tonight,' he continued, 'though I'm not sure you deserve it, if I'm quite honest with you.'

He paused for a moment: 'There's a police helicopter flying from the island to Penzance this evening. And they've found a space for you on it, sonny. The sooner we get you back to your family the better – that's my opinion!'

The policeman rose to his feet, and turned to Martha and Harry.

'Could I ask you a favour? Would you take care of these two bundles of trouble till then?' he said gruffly.

Yes, they replied – they both agreed they could.

'Martha's pie for supper!' said Harry, laughing. 'Worth coming a long way just for a taste of that!'

Chapter 24

William was soon ready to set off back to Hugh Town. He had to organise things and make a report, he said. Jack and Magic were left in Martha's care, while Harry went to see to the milking of his herd of cows, waiting patiently in the barn.

'Tell me about this friend of yours and about your dog.' Martha said when she had taken off her apron and settled into an armchair by the fire. So Jack began to tell her about Charlie going missing, about getting Magic, and how special Magic was; how he could find lost things, and how he was sure Magic could help him find Charlie again.

Martha listened quietly, nodding when Jack described how clever Magic was.

'We don't really understand what goes on in their little heads, do we?' she said. 'I had a really unusual dog when I was a small girl. Always seemed to know what I was thinking. He came everywhere with me, even to school! Waited outside all day for me, he did!' And she looked fondly at Magic, now once again snoring peacefully by the fire.

'And what about Charlie – he must have been a special friend?'

So Jack pulled out from his purse the photo of him and Charlie that he had kept all these months. It was a little damp now from the rain seeping in, and the edges were curling up. Martha leant over to peer at it.

'I'll have to fetch me specs.' she said getting up slowly from her chair. 'Eyesight's not so good now!'

There was a long silence as she took a good look.

'Goodness gracious!' she said at last. 'This lad's not called Charlie Munroe, is he?'

Jack's heart jumped in his throat – he could hardly speak for the surprise.

'Y-y-yes, he is!' he stuttered.

Martha's mouth fell open and she took off her specs and stared at Jack.

'Well, blow me down with a feather!' she exclaimed. 'I can't believe it! Charlie Munroe's living down in Old Town, goes to the little school there. His Mum's a nurse, isn't she?'

Jack couldn't believe his ears. He jumped up and grabbed the sleeping Magic and danced the startled dog in his arms round the room.

'We've done it, we've done it! Magic, Magic, I always knew you'd do it!

The two of them collapsed in a heap on the floor, with Jack laughing with joy and Magic barking with excitement.

'Hold your horses! We'd better check this out, just to be sure.' She paused a moment. 'They won't be in the phone book, will they? They've only been here a few months – we'll have to try directory enquiries. If it's true, that dog of yours is quite some detective!'

Jack was all in a jitter now, but soon Martha had called and was coming back with thumbs up and a big smile. They were in luck: Mrs Munroe was at home, though she was more than a bit shocked, Martha said, so it took some time to explain things. But she was bringing Charlie over as soon as she could.

'It's lucky,' Martha said, 'that St Mary's is so small – only 2000 people here, so everyone knows everyone else.'

And when at last Charlie arrived, there were loud yells of delight from both the boys. It was obvious from the hugs and tears that Charlie had badly missed Jack too. When things had calmed down a bit, they all sat down to Martha's delicious pie supper. And when the plates were all scraped clean, there was stewed apple and custard to follow. Magic, as a reward, had a helping of Martha's pie and lots of gravy. And, Martha said later, Jack and Charlie talked 'nineteen to the dozen' all through the meal. At that moment, there were no happier boys on the island.

Chapter 25

It took some time for the whole story to be untangled. Martha found a quiet moment while they were doing the dishes together, to ask Charlie's mum why she'd left Abingdon.

'It was Charlie's dad, you see,' she said. He'd wanted to take Charlie off with him to Scotland, where they'd all lived when Charlie was small. And he was threatening her and saying he'd take him away, so she got scared. The Scilly Isles seemed a good place to hide, well out of his reach. Martha nodded sympathetically:

'But luckily, not good enough to hide from Magic!' she said, with a laugh.

Jack's journey home began when Harry reminded them they had to be at the airport to get the helicopter. The flight should have been a thrill, but Jack was now so tired he could barely stand.

At the airport, Harry had to carry a sleeping boy from his car into the hands of the police. Magic was exhausted too and soon curled up in a cardboard box on the helicopter's floor.

The welcome home for Jack was a tearful one too; Mr and Mrs Bennett were both sobbing, and even Sally was wiping tears from her eyes. When everything had calmed down a little, it was fixed for Charlie to come over on the boat to stay for the remainder of the holiday. And, for sure, there would be now be plenty of holidays for them both to look forward to.

Magic, the hero now, seemed bemused by all the fuss they made over him. As soon as he could, he dashed straight upstairs and curled himself up on Jack's bed, to dream of Martha's delicious meat pie.

Clare lives in Oxford and is married, with two grown-up children and two grandsons. She enjoys writing stories, and reading to her grandsons, as well as keeping in touch with all her great-nephews and nieces. She loves her garden and has a naughty spaniel called Nip.

Amy can be found at:
www.amybrownillustration.com